Grandpa's Tent

Mary Davila and Sarah Kinney Gaventa
Illustrated by Paul Shaffer

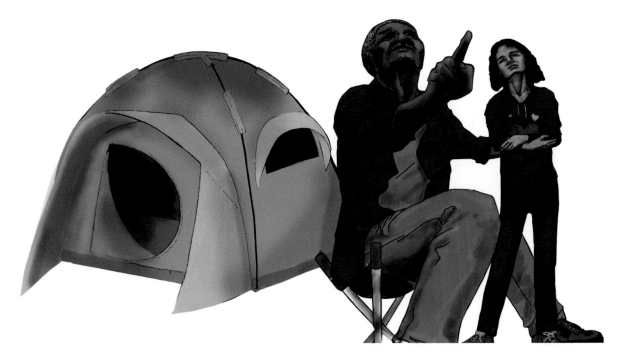

© 2018 Forward Movement

ISBN: 978-0-88028-440-0

Printed in USA

Forward
Movement
inspire disciples. empower evangelists.

Dedication

This book is dedicated to all children, especially Arri and Etta. May you
always be curious, ask questions, and seek to know God more deeply.
I am also grateful for the encouragement of the people of St. James' Episcopal Church,
Leesburg, Virginia, and Christ Church Episcopal, Raleigh, North Carolina.
You have loved me well! Finally, I am most grateful for my biggest
cheerleader, Chris. ~ Mary

To my grandparents and mother, who taught me about death.
And to Matt and Charlie, who brighten every day of my life. ~ Sarah

Families have different summer traditions. Some families go to the beach. Some families go to big cities. Some families travel to visit relatives.

Hannah's family went camping in the mountains. While her parents parked the car, Hannah and Grandpa walked to the campsite to select a perfect place for their tent. Grandpa liked to wake up to see the sun sparkling on the water. Hannah liked the sound of birds and frogs cooing her to sleep.

Grandpa and Hannah always put up the tent together.

When Hannah was three years old, Grandpa held her hands as she scooped up prickly pine needles to clear a space for the tent. When she was four, he trusted her to steady the pegs as he hammered them into the ground. The next year, Grandpa invited her to hold the tent while he put the frame in place, and Hannah felt very grown up.

Each year, Hannah learned more from Grandpa—about camping and other important things too. Being in the forest always made Grandpa feel closer to God, and he liked to tell Hannah stories from the Bible. Her favorite stories were about Jesus. Jesus loved everybody: little children, grumpy disciples, and the people who came to hear him speak.

Hannah and Grandpa talked about everything. Grandpa did his best to answer all of Hannah's questions. One evening as they sat around the campfire, Hannah asked about Grandma.

"Mom told me that Grandma is in heaven," Hannah said. "But I'm not sure what heaven is."

Grandpa thought for a minute. "Well, Hannah, everything that is alive eventually dies. To die means your heart stops beating, your lungs stop breathing, and your brain stops working."

"And then what happens?" asked Hannah.

"Well, our bodies are buried, but we go on living forever in heaven."

Hannah felt confused.

"Maybe I can explain death and heaven like this," Grandpa said. "Every summer, we put up this tent together, right?"

"Yes," said Hannah.

"Do we live in the tent forever, or do we just stay here for a few days?"

Hannah answered, "We stay here for a few days, and then we go back home."

"Exactly," said Grandpa. "When we finish camping, we pack up the tent and put it away. In the Bible, Saint Paul says our bodies are like tents. In biblical times, many people lived in tents so they understood when Saint Paul explained heaven and life like a tent. We live in these tents for a little while, but eventually we go home—we go to heaven to be with God."

"What is heaven like?" Hannah asked.

Grandpa said, "No one knows exactly what heaven is like, but the Bible gives us some clues. Jesus tells us that heaven is a place that God has specially prepared for us. In heaven everyone worships God. There are no tears in heaven and no darkness, only light. Heaven is full of celebration and laughter."

The next summer, Grandpa couldn't go camping with Hannah and her parents. He had moved into a nursing home, and he wasn't feeling very well.

Hannah and her mother visited Grandpa in his new home. Hannah's mom told her that most of the people at the nursing home were older like Grandpa, and some needed extra help with eating and walking. Hannah was nervous.

She didn't like the way the nursing home smelled, and she felt uncomfortable seeing all the people in wheelchairs.

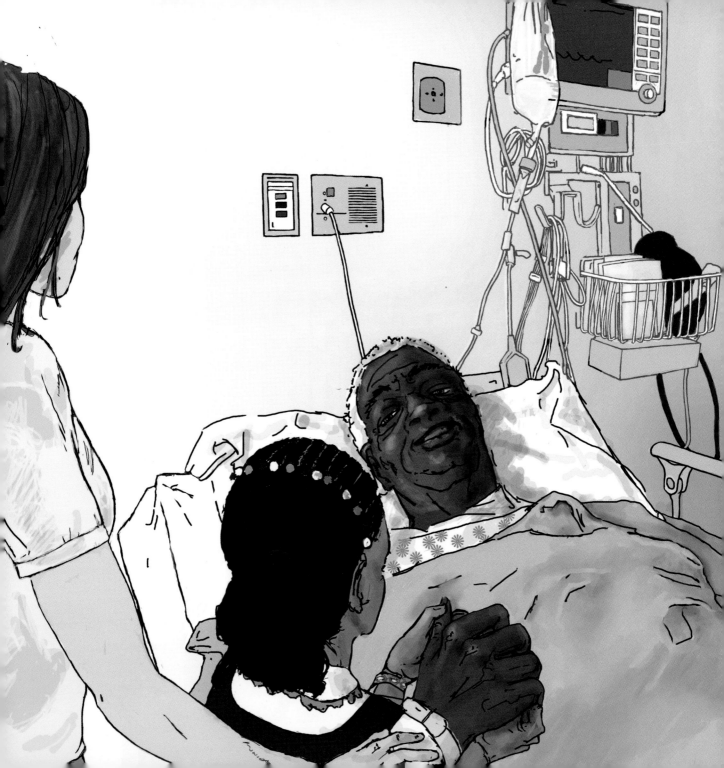

Hannah's hands started to shake when she saw Grandpa in his bed. He looked so weak and sick. But when he opened his eyes and saw Hannah, Grandpa's face beamed.

"When can we go camping again, Grandpa?" Hannah asked.

Grandpa smiled and took Hannah's hand in his. "Do you remember how I told you that our bodies are like tents? Well, my tent isn't as strong as it used to be, and I'm not sure I will be able to go camping again. But, oh, how I have loved camping with you." Hannah started to cry and laid her head on Grandpa's shoulder.

"Hannah, I am so thankful for our camping adventures," Grandpa said. "I will always remember those special times, and I hope you will too. My body is growing weaker, but I am okay. I have you and your parents and God, surrounding me with love." Hannah hugged Grandpa.

"I love you, Grandpa."

"I love you too, Hannah."

A few weeks later, Hannah's parents were waiting at the school bus stop for Hannah. They walked home together, and when they came inside the house, her father knelt down and held Hannah's shoulders. "Hannah, I am so sorry to tell you this, but Grandpa died this afternoon. His heart stopped beating, and his lungs stopped breathing."

Hannah's mother told her that Grandpa had left a special gift for her and gave her a big, beautiful box. Inside was the tent that they used for camping. Hannah started to cry. Her mother hugged her and reminded her about how much Grandpa enjoyed camping with her. The tent was a gift to help her remember those special times.

That night, Hannah prayed: "Dear God, I know Grandpa will be okay because you will take very good care of him. But I am going to miss him so much, and I wish we could go camping again! Please, if you could, give him a hug for me."

The next morning, Mother Lucy, Grandpa's priest, came to the house to help Hannah's parents plan the funeral. Hannah had never been to a funeral before.

Mother Lucy explained, "A funeral is a time to give thanks for your Grandpa's life and to celebrate his new life in heaven. We will have a special service at the church, and then we'll bury his body in the cemetery."

Hannah asked, "Where is Grandpa now?"

Hannah's mother said, "Grandpa's body is at the funeral home, but Grandpa is in heaven."

Hannah nervously asked if she would see Grandpa's body.

"Yes," said her mother. "You can see his body at the funeral home. You don't need to be afraid. Grandpa's body will be in a special box called a casket. Grandpa's body will look like the Grandpa you remember, only his body won't have life in it. It is like a tent without sleeping bags or lanterns or other supplies."

Mother Lucy asked Hannah if she had any questions.

"Grandpa explained heaven to me and how our bodies are like tents until we go to be with God. I know that God will take good care of Grandpa in heaven, but I really wish he were here with me. Why do people have to die?"

Mother Lucy nodded her head. "It is very hard to lose someone. But our bodies aren't made to live forever. Saying goodbye to someone we love is very sad, but we know that Grandpa is safe in God's hands, and that we will always remember him and how special he was to us."

Mother Lucy suggested that Hannah color a picture that reminded her of Grandpa. Hannah knew just what she wanted to draw: a tent.

The next few days were hard but also a little fun. While Hannah was very sad and missed her Grandpa, she also saw her cousins and aunts and uncles who had traveled to town for the funeral.

Hannah and her parents went to the funeral home for the visitation. Her parents explained that this was a time for friends and family to visit with each other. Grandpa's body was there in a casket. Grandpa was dressed in his finest suit, but there was no life in him. He didn't look like the happy and smiling Grandpa that Hannah remembered. She placed the picture of the tent on top of the casket, and Hannah cried for a few minutes.

The next day, Hannah went to the funeral at Grandpa's church. Hannah sat with her family in the front of the church close to the casket, which was covered by a beautiful white cloth called a pall. Hannah's mother read a passage from the Bible about how there will be no more tears in heaven. Grandpa's best friend told funny stories about Grandpa.

Mother Lucy talked about how much Grandpa loved his family—especially his camping trips with Hannah. Mother Lucy also talked about how much God loves us and how Grandpa's life continues on in heaven with God.

After Mother Lucy's sermon, everyone sang one of Grandpa's favorite hymns, "Amazing Grace." Mother Lucy said the prayers, and then she invited everyone to receive Holy Communion, which she said helped everyone understand what it was like to join in the heavenly feast, sitting around a table with God.

Mother Lucy stood by the casket and reminded everyone that God is more powerful than death. She asked God to give Grandpa peace and rest and to comfort the hearts of everyone who missed him.

After the church part of the funeral service, everyone walked to the cemetery to bury Grandpa's body. Hannah saw some people carrying the casket to a big hole. Hannah noticed lots of stones with people's names written on them. Hannah's mother explained that each stone marked the place where a person's body had been buried. Her mother said that Hannah could come back and visit Grandpa's grave and bring flowers or a special drawing.

Mother Lucy said some more prayers, and she invited everyone to put a handful of earth's soil on top of the casket. Hannah held her mother's hand when she realized her mother was crying. Hannah started to cry too, because she missed Grandpa so much.

Mother Lucy invited Hannah and her parents to have a quiet moment by the grave, and then everyone went back to the church for a reception.

Lots of people gave Hannah hugs and told her how wonderful Grandpa was. She noticed how many people brought food and had kind words to say. Their kindness made Hannah feel better.

Hannah missed Grandpa a lot, even after she went back to school, even after weeks had passed. Sometimes, when she said her nighttime prayers, she told Jesus how much she missed her Grandpa and asked Jesus to say hello for her.

Hannah's mom noticed that Hannah was feeling sad and told her, "Hannah, it's okay to cry because you miss Grandpa. What do you think about spending some time in your tent? We can set it up in the backyard and sleep in it tonight."

Hannah helped her parents set up the tent, just like she had helped Grandpa. That night, as she looked at the stars, she imagined Grandpa in heaven, smiling at her.

Hannah knew that Grandpa was safe with God in his permanent home in heaven. And she knew that the love they shared would live in her heart forever.

Note to Parents

Talking with children about the death of a loved one can feel like a difficult task. In the past, children were often sheltered from knowledge or discussions of death. Children who have lost a loved one cope better throughout their lives if they have been given a chance to work through their feelings of grief. We hope this book will be a helpful tool for children and those who love them to talk about death and grief.

As pastors, we are often asked questions about talking with children about death and funerals. Listed below are some talking points and rituals we have found to be helpful.

Before the Funeral

Children often ask poignant, heartfelt, direct questions about death and heaven. It's okay not to have all of the answers—no one does! We encourage families to continue the conversation and to speak honestly. It's helpful to use direct language such as "death" instead of "pass away" and to avoid language that speaks of death as "resting." That can be confusing for a child.

Cremation is becoming a more commonly used form of burial. Children may have questions about cremation. We can remind them that just as God created humans from the dust, so do our bodies return to the dust when we die.

During the Funeral

You may wonder whether it is appropriate to bring your children to the funeral service. Again, you know your children best, but being present for the funeral and burial can help children understand the concrete nature of death. The same rituals that are important for adults are important for children as well. You can also choose to have your child attend only a portion of the funeral, if you are afraid the length may be too much for him or her. You might also ask older children whether they would like to attend.

Art and writing can be helpful ways for children to express emotions. Perhaps children's art can be displayed in the reception area, or the child can journal privately about his or her questions and memories of the deceased. Children can write letters to the deceased to be placed on top of the casket. Some people also have a tradition of placing flowers or earth on top of the casket. Children can be included in this ritual.

After the Service

Parents may have questions about how much of their own grief their children should witness. Again, trust your own judgment on this, but do not be afraid to shed tears or express sadness in front of your children. This only affirms that their own grief is valid and normal. If you find yourself unable to eat, sleep, or be motivated for ordinary life for months after the death of a loved one, please speak with your physician. Grief can sometimes turn into depression.

Death, appropriately, interrupts daily routines. However, once a family returns home or the funeral service is over, returning to normal routines may help children feel safe and rooted in something stable.

Children (like adults) can mask their sadness and fear and appear "fine." We encourage you to check in with your children periodically about their feelings of grief to give them an opportunity to express how they are really feeling.

Descriptions of Heaven

"(God) will wipe every tear from their eyes. Death will be no more; mourning and crying and pain will be no more."
Revelation 21:4

"In my Father's house there are many dwelling places. If it were not so, would I have told you that I go to prepare a place for you?" John 14:2

"On this mountain the LORD of hosts will make for all peoples a feast of rich food, a feast of well-aged wines, of rich food filled with marrow, of well-aged wines strained clear." Isaiah 25:6

"And the city has no need of sun or moon to shine on it, for the glory of God is its light, and its lamp is the Lamb. The nations will walk by its light, and the kings of the earth will bring their glory into it. Its gates will never be shut by day—and there will be no night there."
Revelation 21:22-25

"After this I looked, and there was a great multitude that no one could count, from every nation, from all tribes and peoples and languages, standing before the throne and before the Lamb, robed in white, with palm branches in their hands. They cried out in a loud voice, saying, "Salvation belongs to our God who is seated on the throne, and to the Lamb!" Revelation 7:9-10

"For we know that if the earthly tent we live in is destroyed, we have a building from God, a house not made with hands, eternal in the heavens. For in this tent we groan, longing to be clothed with our heavenly dwelling—if indeed, when we have taken it off we will not be found naked. For while we are still in this tent, we groan under our burden, because we wish not to be unclothed but to be further clothed, so that what is mortal may be swallowed up by life. He who has prepared us for this very thing is God, who has given us the Spirit as a guarantee. So we are always confident; even though we know that while we are at home in the body we are away from the Lord—for we walk by faith, not by sight. Yes, we do have confidence, and we would rather be away from the body and at home with the Lord."
2 Corinthians 5:1-8

About the Authors and Artist

Mary Davila and her husband, Chris, have two young daughters, Arri and Etta. They live in Raleigh, North Carolina, where Mary is an Episcopal priest and serves as an assistant to the rector at Christ Church.

Sarah Kinney Gaventa is an Episcopal priest and serves as the dean of students at Austin Presbyterian Theological Seminary. She lives in Austin, Texas, with her husband, Matthew, and son, Charlie.

Paul Shaffer is a retired Episcopal priest and an artist who lives in Brooklyn Center, Minnesota.

About Forward Movement

Forward Movement inspires disciples and empowers evangelists. We live out our ministry by publishing books, daily reflections, studies for small groups, and online resources. We encourage families to visit www.GrowChristians.org, a Forward Movement website devoted to helping adults and children grow together in faith. Our daily devotion, *Forward Day by Day*, is also available in Spanish (*Adelante Día a Día*) and Braille, online, as a podcast, and as an app for smartphones or tablets. A ministry of the Episcopal Church for more than eighty years, Forward Movement is a nonprofit organization funded by sales of resources and gifts from generous donors.

To learn more about Forward Movement and our resources, please visit www.ForwardMovement.org. We are delighted to be doing this work and invite your prayers and support.